W9-AKB-344

DATE DUE

MR 7'86	JE 09'90	OC 18'90	JL 29'96
AP 4'86	JY 14'90	FE 1'91	JL 17'96
AP 22'86	AP 6'89	FE 22'91	MY 14'9
NO 11'86	MY 8'89	MY 25'91	MAY 1 3 '98
	MY 30'89	AG 7'01	AG 0 4 '98
JA 13'87	AG 22'88		
AG 20'87	JE 6'90	AG 23'9	OC 01 '99
NO 23'8	JY 19'90	NO 11'9	MR 27 '00
JA 23'88	JY 25'90	MY 20'92	SE 25 '0
AP 19'88	JY 30'90	JE 3'99	JE 03 02
MY 16'88	AG 16'90	MAY 31 9	MY 13 '05
MY 31'88	AG 31'90	JUN 19 96	

MY 26 '0
AG 7 1 7

E
Mot   Mother Goose
           Little Boy Blue and
           other favorites

This book belongs to

_____

MOTHER GOOSE'S NURSERY RHYMES

LITTLE BOY BLUE
AND OTHER FAVORITES

ILLUSTRATED BY
ALLEN ATKINSON

AN ARIEL BOOK

BANTAM BOOKS
TORONTO · NEW YORK · LONDON · SYDNEY · AUCKLAND

LITTLE BOY BLUE AND OTHER FAVORITES
A Bantam Book
April 1985

Art Direction: Armand Eisen and Tom Durwood

ISBN 0-553-15320-X

Published simultaneously in the United States and Canada

Bantam Books are published by Bantam Books, Inc. Its trademark,
consisting of the words "Bantam Books" and the portrayal of a rooster, is
Registered in U.S. Patent and Trademark Office and in other countries.
Marca Registrada. Bantam Books, Inc., 666 Fifth Avenue, New York,
New York 10103.

Printing and binding by
Printer, industria gráfica S.A.   Provenza, 388   Barcelona
Depósito legal B. 333-1985
PRINTED IN SPAIN
0 9 8 7 6 5 4 3 2 1

"No, no, my melodies will never die,
While nurses sing or babies cry."
—Mother Goose

LITTLE BOY BLUE, come blow your horn,
The sheep's in the meadow, the cow's in the corn.
But where is the little boy who looks after the sheep?
He's under the haystack fast asleep.
Will you wake him? No, not I,
For if I do, he's sure to cry.

THIS IS THE HOUSE that Jack built.

MOTHER GOOSE'S NURSERY RHYMES

This is the malt
That lay in the house that Jack built.

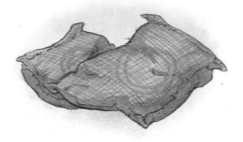

This is the rat,
That ate the malt
That lay in the house that Jack built.

13

This is the cat,
That killed the rat,
That ate the malt
That lay in the house that Jack built.

This is the dog,
That worried the cat,
That killed the rat,
That ate the malt
That lay in the house that Jack built.

This is the cow with the crumpled horn,
That tossed the dog,
That worried the cat,
That killed the rat,
That ate the malt
That lay in the house that Jack built.

This is the maiden all forlorn,
That milked the cow with the crumpled horn,
That tossed the dog,
That worried the cat,
That killed the rat,
That ate the malt
That lay in the house that Jack built.

This is the man all tattered and torn,
That kissed the maiden all forlorn,
That milked the cow with the crumpled horn,
That tossed the dog,
That worried the cat,
That killed the rat,
That ate the malt
That lay in the house that Jack built.

This is the priest all shaven and shorn,
That married the man all tattered and torn,
That kissed the maiden all forlorn,
That milked the cow with the crumpled horn,
That tossed the dog,
That worried the cat,
That killed the rat,
That ate the malt
That lay in the house that Jack built.

This is the cock that crowed in the morn,
That waked the priest all shaven and shorn,
That married the man all tattered and torn,
That kissed the maiden all forlorn,
That milked the cow with the crumpled horn,
That tossed the dog,
That worried the cat,
That killed the rat,
That ate the malt
That lay in the house that Jack built.

This is the farmer sowing his corn,
That kept the cock that crowed in the morn,
That waked the priest all shaven and shorn,
That married the man all tattered and torn,
That kissed the maiden all forlorn,
That milked the cow with the crumpled horn,
That tossed the dog,
That worried the cat,
That killed the rat,
That ate the malt
That lay in the house that Jack built.

ITSY BITSY SPIDER
climbed up the water spout,

Down came the rain
and washed
poor
spider
out.

Out came the sun,
      and dried up all the rain;

And the itsy bitsy spider
climbed up
the spout
again.

SEE-SAW, Margery Daw,
Jacky shall have a new master;
Jacky must have but a penny a day,
Because he can't work any faster.

THERE WAS AN old woman
Lived under a hill,
And if she isn't gone,
She lives there still.

Baked apples she sold,
And cranberry pies,
And she's the old woman
That never told lies.

I LOVE SIXPENCE, jolly little sixpence
I love sixpence better than my life.
I spent a penny of it, I lent a penny of it,
And I took fourpence home to my wife.

Oh, my little fourpence, jolly little fourpence,
I love fourpence better than my life.
I spent a penny of it, I lent a penny of it,
And I took twopence home to my wife.

Oh, my little twopence, jolly little twopence,
I love twopence better than my life.
I spent a penny of it, I lent a penny of it,
And I took nothing home to my wife.

Oh, my little nothing, jolly little nothing,
What will nothing buy for my wife?
I have nothing, I spend nothing,
I love nothing better than my wife.

TWEEDLEDUM and Tweedledee
Agreed to fight a battle,
For Tweedledum said Tweedledee
Had spoiled his nice new rattle.
Just then flew by a monstrous crow,
As black as a tar-barrel,
Which frightened both the heroes so,
They quite forgot their quarrel.

MOTHER GOOSE'S NURSERY RHYMES

RING AROUND the rosie,
A pocket full of posies;
Ashes, ashes!
We all fall down.

IF WISHES were horses
Beggars would ride;
If turnips were watches
I would wear one by my side.
And if "ifs" and "ands" were pots and pans,
There'd be no work for tinkers!

MOTHER GOOSE'S NURSERY RHYMES

FOR WANT OF A NAIL the shoe was lost,
For want of a shoe the horse was lost,
For want of a horse the rider was lost,
For want of a rider the battle was lost,
For want of a battle the kingdom was lost,
And all for the want of a horseshoe nail.

LITTLE Tommy Tucker
Sings for his supper.
What shall he eat?
Brown bread and butter.
How will he cut it,
Without e'er a knife?
And how will he be married,
Without e'er a wife?

DING DONG BELL
Pussy's in the well.
Who put her in?
Little Johnny Green.
Who pulled her out?
Little Tommy Stout.
What a naughty boy was that
To try to drown poor pussycat,
Who never did any harm,
And killed the mice in his father's barn.

IF I'D AS MUCH money as I could spend,
I never would cry, Old chairs to mend.
Old chairs to mend! Old chairs to mend!
I never would cry, Old chairs to mend.

If I'd as much money as I could tell,
I never would cry, Old clothes to sell.
Old clothes to sell! Old clothes to sell!
I never would cry, Old clothes to sell.

LADYBUG, ladybug,
Fly away home,
Your house is on fire,
Your children will burn.

IF YOU LOVE ME, love me true,
Send me a ribbon, and let it be blue.
If you hate me, let it be seen,
Send me a ribbon, a ribbon of green.

TWINKLE, twinkle, little star
How I wonder what you are!
Up above the world so high,
Like a diamond in the sky.

MOTHER GOOSE'S NURSERY RHYMES

ABOUT THE ILLUSTRATOR

Allen Atkinson is one of America's most beloved illustrators, whose works include *The Tale of Peter Rabbit* and other tales by Beatrix Potter, *The Velveteen Rabbit*, and *Mother Goose's Nursery Rhymes*, among others. Mr. Atkinson lives in rural Connecticut, where he was born and raised. His favorite subjects for his paintings are the well-known children's stories which he read as a child. In addition to book illustrations he enjoys creating toys for children.

Allen Atkinson has designed four charming stuffed bean-bag toys: Humpty Dumpty, Little Miss Muffet, Simple Simon, and a mouse from Three Blind Mice, all based on his artwork in *Mother Goose's Nursery Rhymes*. For information, write to The Toy Works, Box 48, Middle Falls, N.Y. 12848.